WHERE'S WALDO?
THE COLORING BOOK

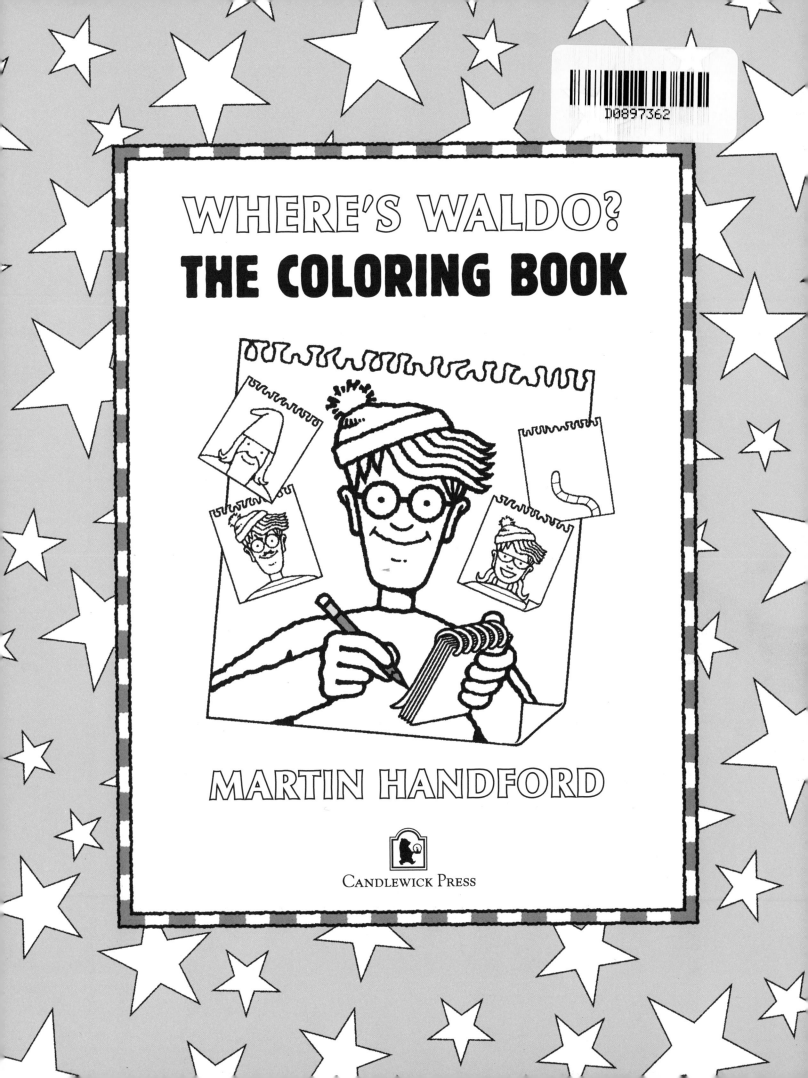

MARTIN HANDFORD

CANDLEWICK PRESS

HOW-DE-DOODLE, WALDO FANS!

BRING THE PAGES OF THIS BOOK TO LIFE BY COLORING THEM IN. WOW! BUT THAT'S NOT ALL, WALDO-WATCHERS! FIND ME IN EVERY SCENE (IT'S EVEN TRICKIER IN BLACK AND WHITE!). THEN SEE IF YOU CAN ALSO SPOT ONE OF MY LOST PENCILS IN EACH OF THE PLACES I'VE VISITED.

BUT THE FUN DOESN'T STOP THERE! I'VE ALSO LOST SKETCHES I MADE OF MY KEY, WOOF'S BONE, WENDA'S CAMERA, WIZARD WHITEBEARD'S SCROLL, AND ODLAW'S BINOCULARS. EACH ONE APPEARS ONLY ONCE!

NOW GET SEARCHING AS YOU COLOR—OFF WE GO!

Waldo

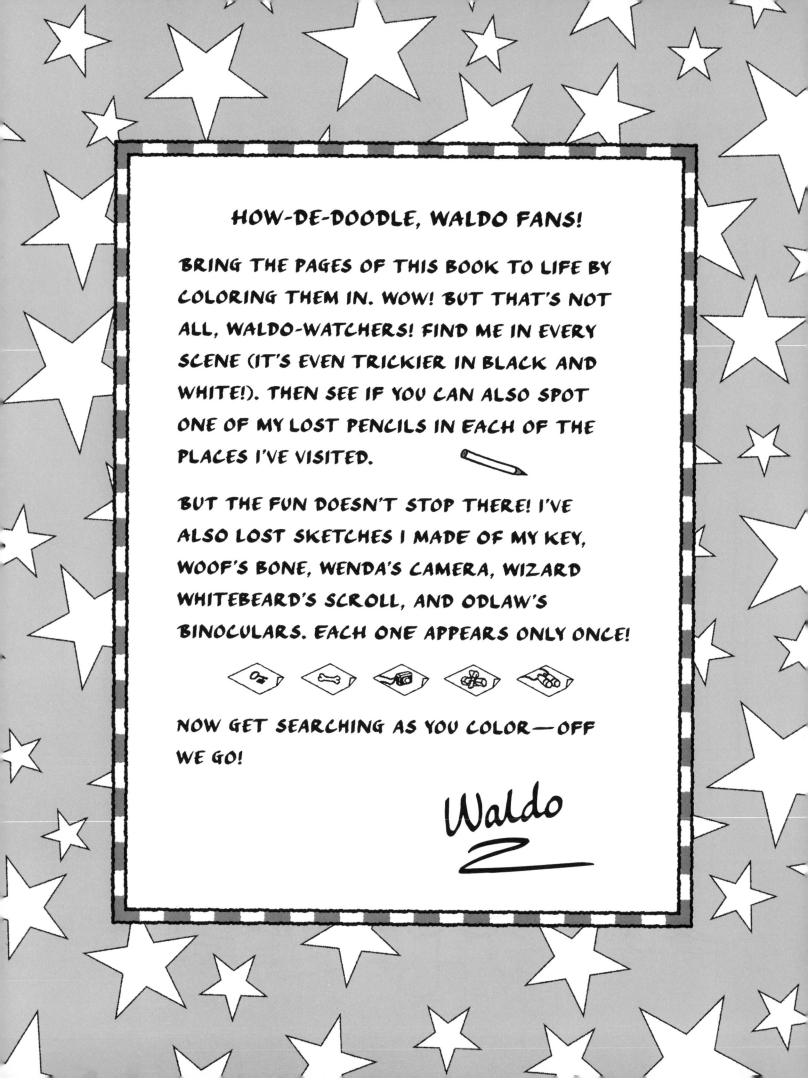

THESE BOOKS HAVE COME ALIVE! FANTASTIC!

WHY NOT ADD YOUR OWN BOOK TITLES?

CREATE AS MANY CRAZY CAKE COLORS AS YOU CAN!

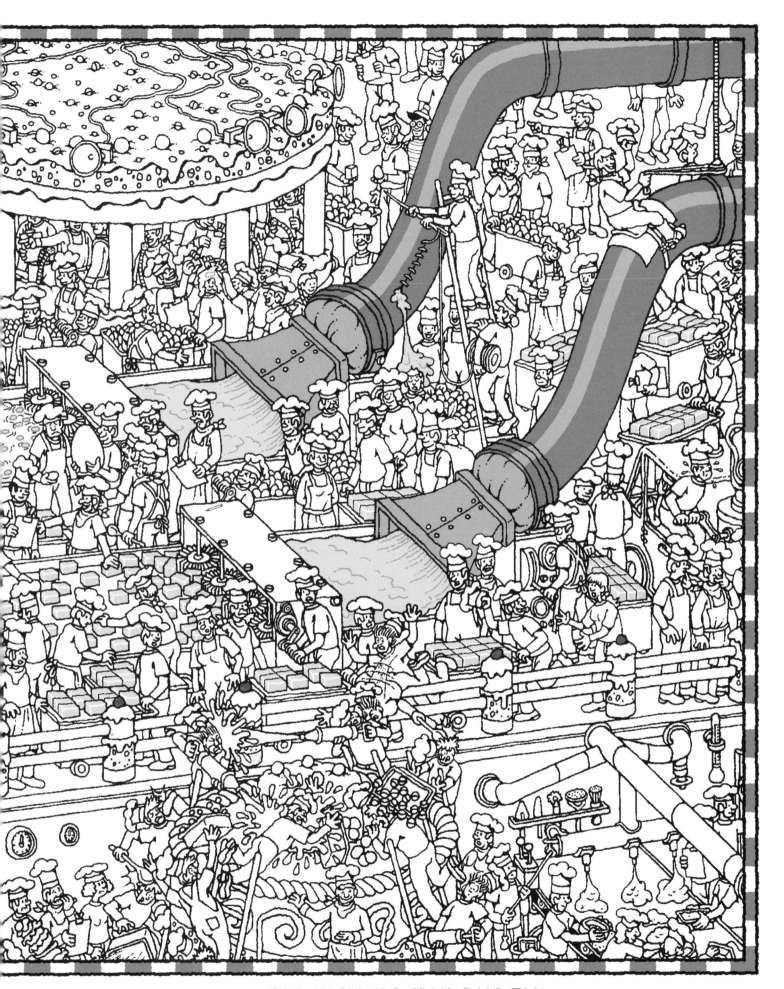

FIND AN EGG-AND-SPOON RACE, TOO!

ARE STRAWBERRIES RED AND BANANAS YELLOW? THEY DON'T HAVE TO BE!

CLAP YOUR HANDS! SHUFFLE YOUR FEET! COLOR IN THE CONGA LINES!

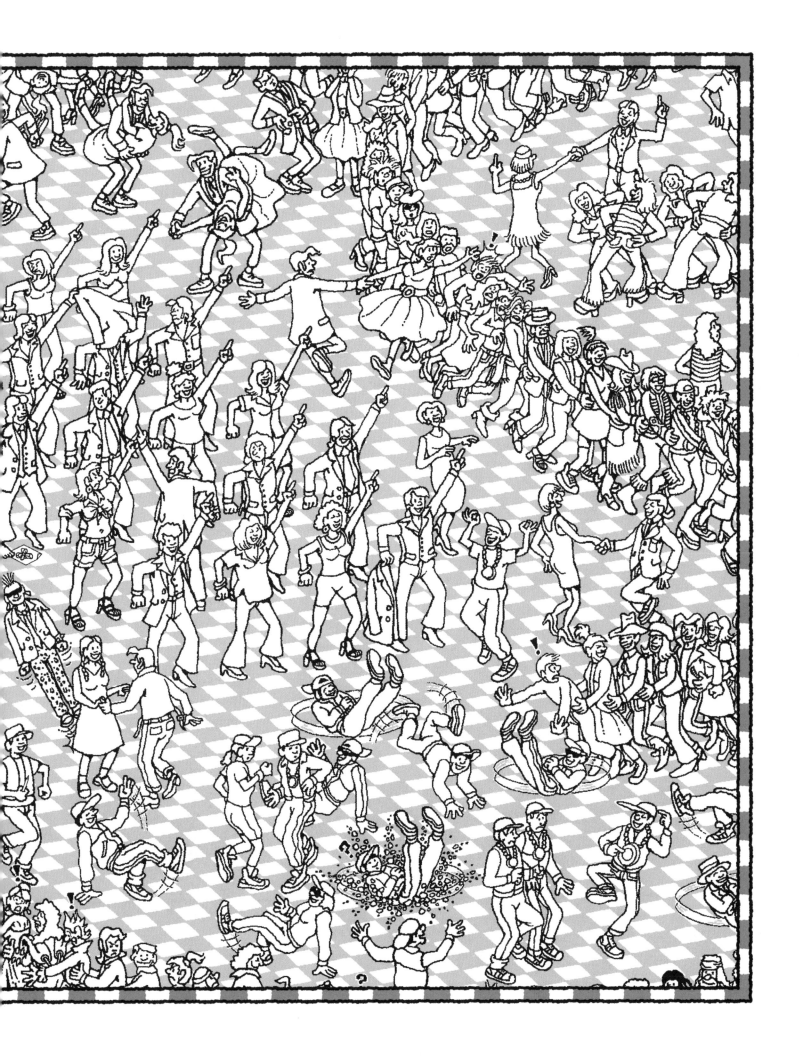

FIND BAND MEMBERS DRESSED AS BEARS, PIGS, BIRDS, CROCODILES, AND BULLS!

GIVE SOME WALDO-WATCHERS STRIPED TOPS (OR ANY OTHER DESIGN YOU LIKE)!

CAN YOU ALSO SPOT ONE HAT MISSING A POM-POM?

WHAT COLORS DO FLYING MONSTERS COME IN?

WHY NOT DRAW A SLIPPERY SEA EEL AROUND THE FRAME?

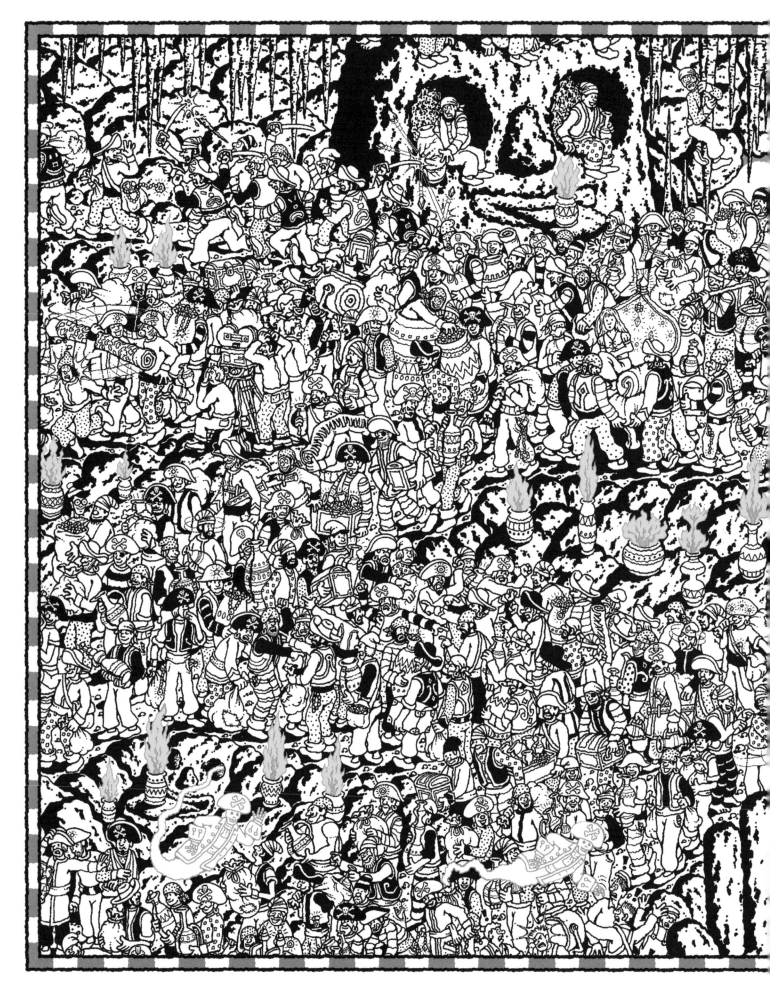

ADD SOME MAGIC SPARKLE TO THIS SHINY TREASURE TROVE!

AND SHIVER ME TIMBERS! SEARCH FOR THREE PIRATE GHOSTS!

TOYS CAN BE AS COLORFUL AS A RAINBOW! WHAT DO YOU IMAGINE?

ALSO SEARCH FOR A TEDDY BEAR FLYING A PAPER PLANE!

FILL THE WHITE BORDER WITH DOODLES OF DINOSAUR BONES! HOW MANY CAN YOU FIT?

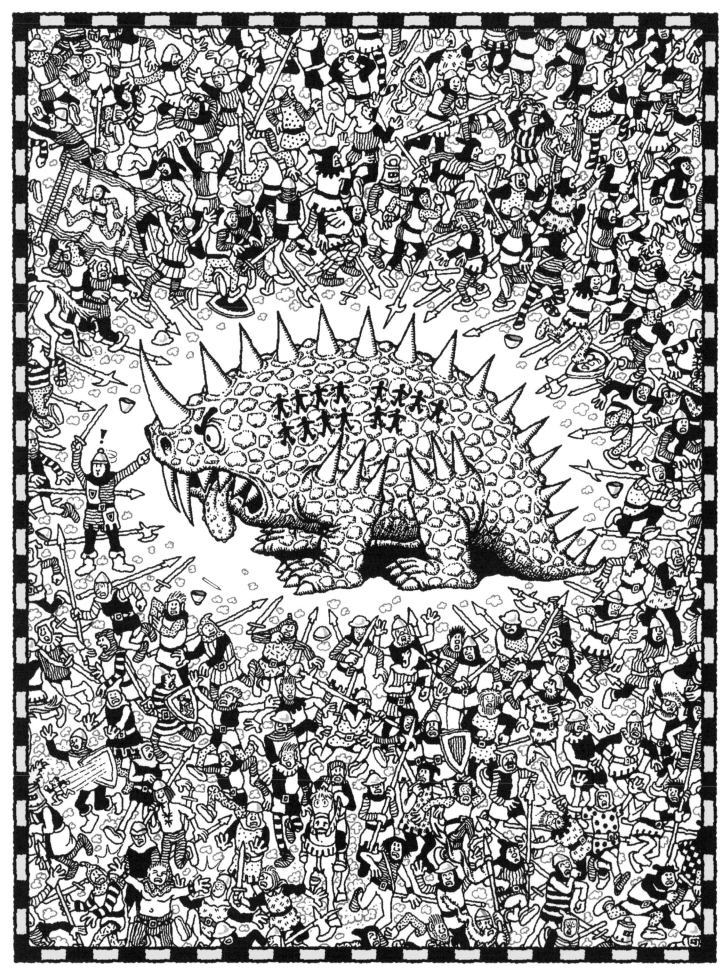

WALDO'S IN THIS PICTURE BUT NOT IN ANY OF THE FOUR OPPOSITE.

THINK UP NAMES FOR ODLAW'S FIERCE FRIENDS AND SEEK OUT AN ODLAW COIN!

ADD MUDDY, SWAMPY FOOTPRINTS AROUND THE FRAME!

USE A MERRY MISHMASH OF COLORS FOR THE SHIELDS, TENTS, AND FLAGS!

CAN YOU SPOT ROBIN HOOD?

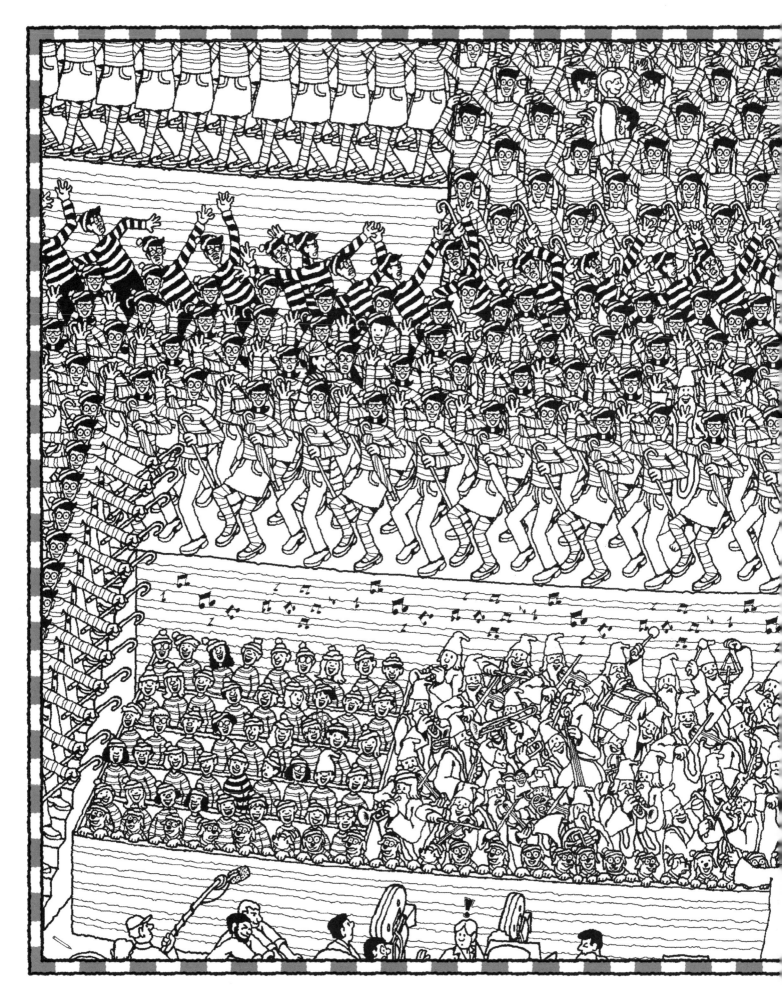

LOOK AT ALL THE PEOPLE DRESSED UP AS US!

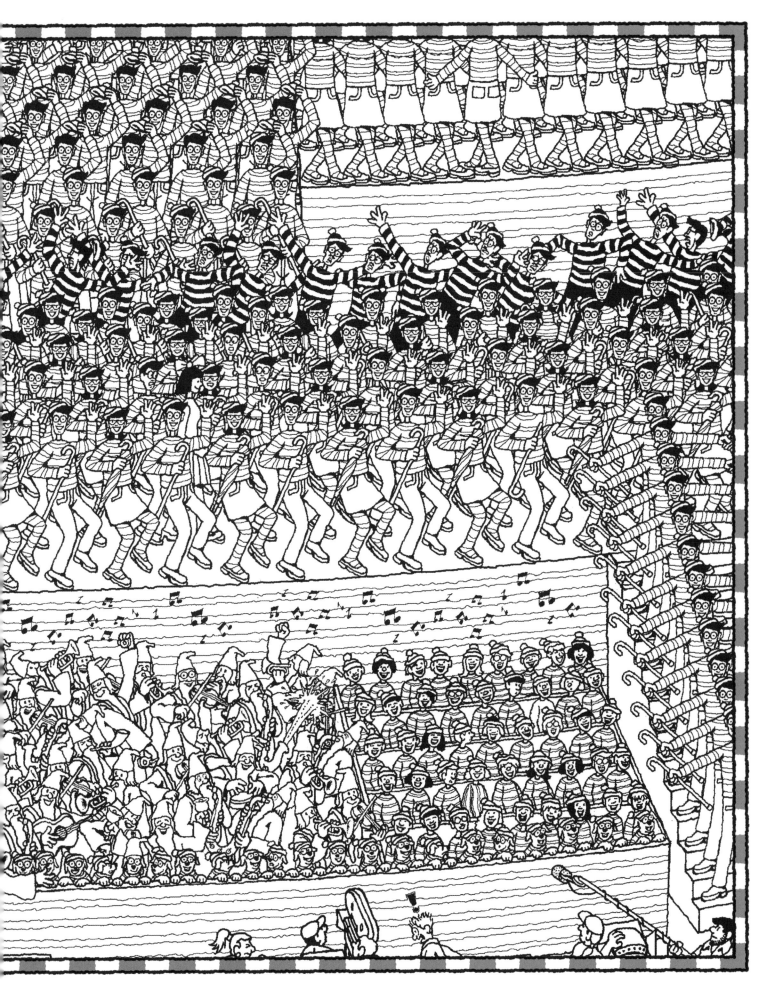

I'M THE ONE HOLDING MY WALKING STICK UPSIDE DOWN.

HERE ARE CHECKLISTS WITH MORE THINGS FOR YOU TO SEARCH FOR. WHY NOT ADD YOUR OWN CHECKLIST ITEMS IN THE BLANK SPACES? HAVE FUN!

George washing ton

Hamlet making an omelet

Whistling Whistler painting his mother

The Pilgrim fathers

....

....

A buffalo **stamp**ede

Calamity Jane

A horse being shoed

A couple of gunslingers

....

....

A butter chef

A chef slipping on butter

An egg juggler

An "egg" head

....

....

A concussed dragon

Lines at two bus dragon stops

An accidental slap in the face

A dragon with a very long tail

....

....

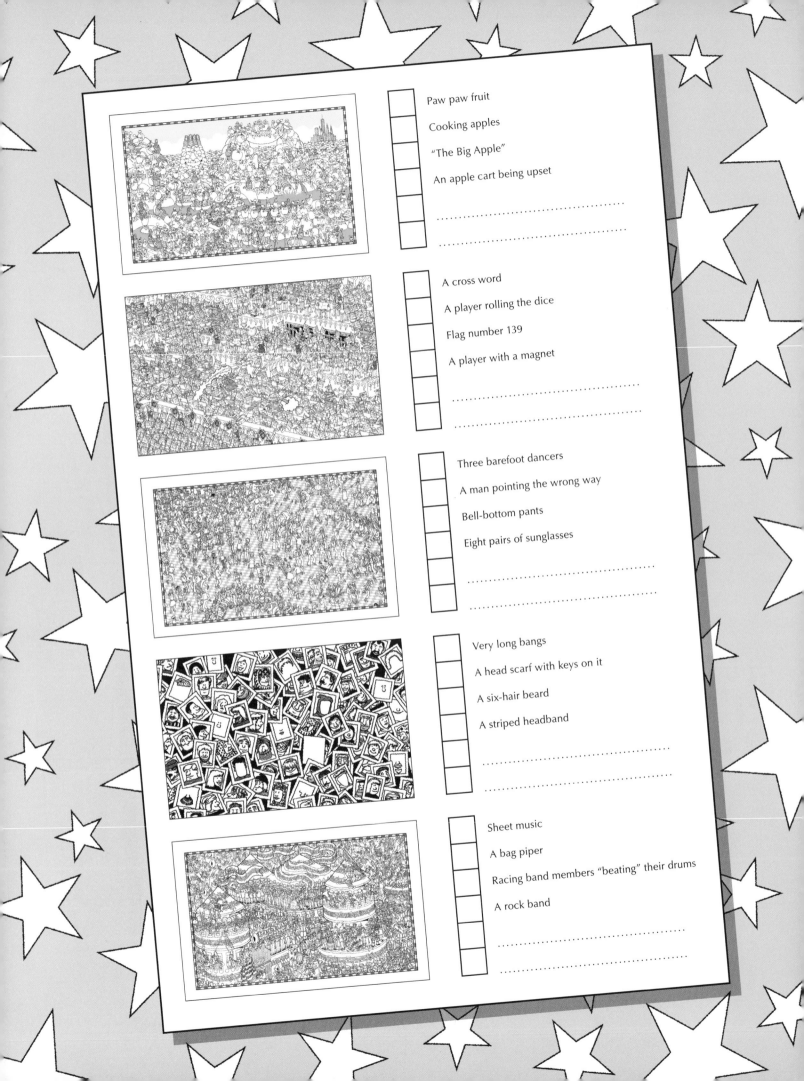

Paw paw fruit

Cooking apples

"The Big Apple"

An apple cart being upset

....

....

A cross word

A player rolling the dice

Flag number 139

A player with a magnet

....

....

Three barefoot dancers

A man pointing the wrong way

Bell-bottom pants

Eight pairs of sunglasses

....

....

Very long bangs

A head scarf with keys on it

A six-hair beard

A striped headband

....

....

Sheet music

A bag piper

Racing band members "beating" their drums

A rock band

....

....

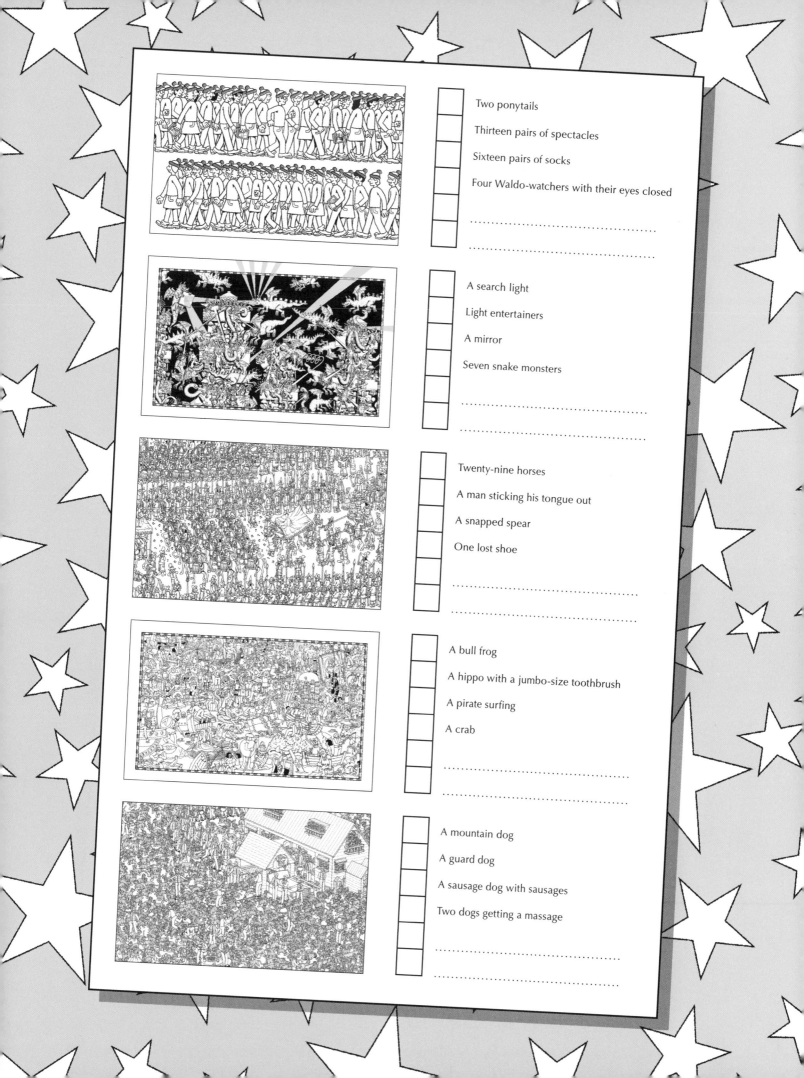

Two ponytails

Thirteen pairs of spectacles

Sixteen pairs of socks

Four Waldo-watchers with their eyes closed

....

....

A search light

Light entertainers

A mirror

Seven snake monsters

....

....

Twenty-nine horses

A man sticking his tongue out

A snapped spear

One lost shoe

....

....

A bull frog

A hippo with a jumbo-size toothbrush

A pirate surfing

A crab

....

....

A mountain dog

A guard dog

A sausage dog with sausages

Two dogs getting a massage

....

....

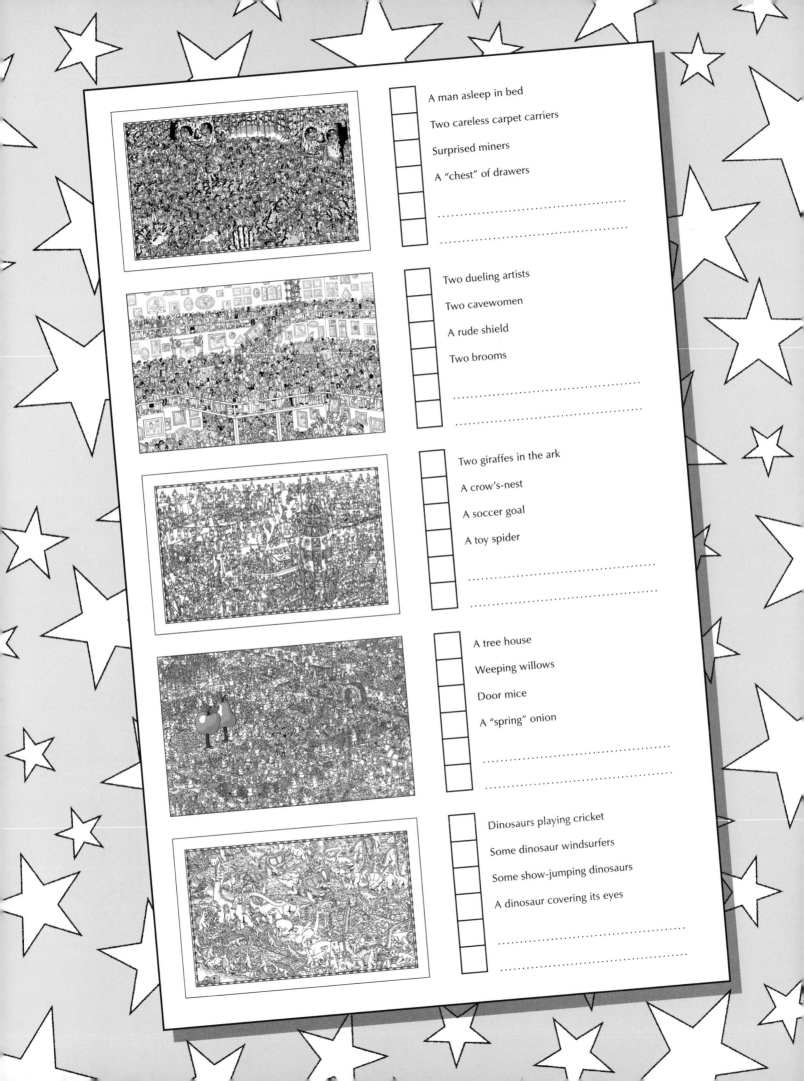

A man asleep in bed

Two careless carpet carriers

Surprised miners

A "chest" of drawers

....

....

Two dueling artists

Two cavewomen

A rude shield

Two brooms

....

....

Two giraffes in the ark

A crow's-nest

A soccer goal

A toy spider

....

....

A tree house

Weeping willows

Door mice

A "spring" onion

....

....

Dinosaurs playing cricket

Some dinosaur windsurfers

Some show-jumping dinosaurs

A dinosaur covering its eyes

....

....

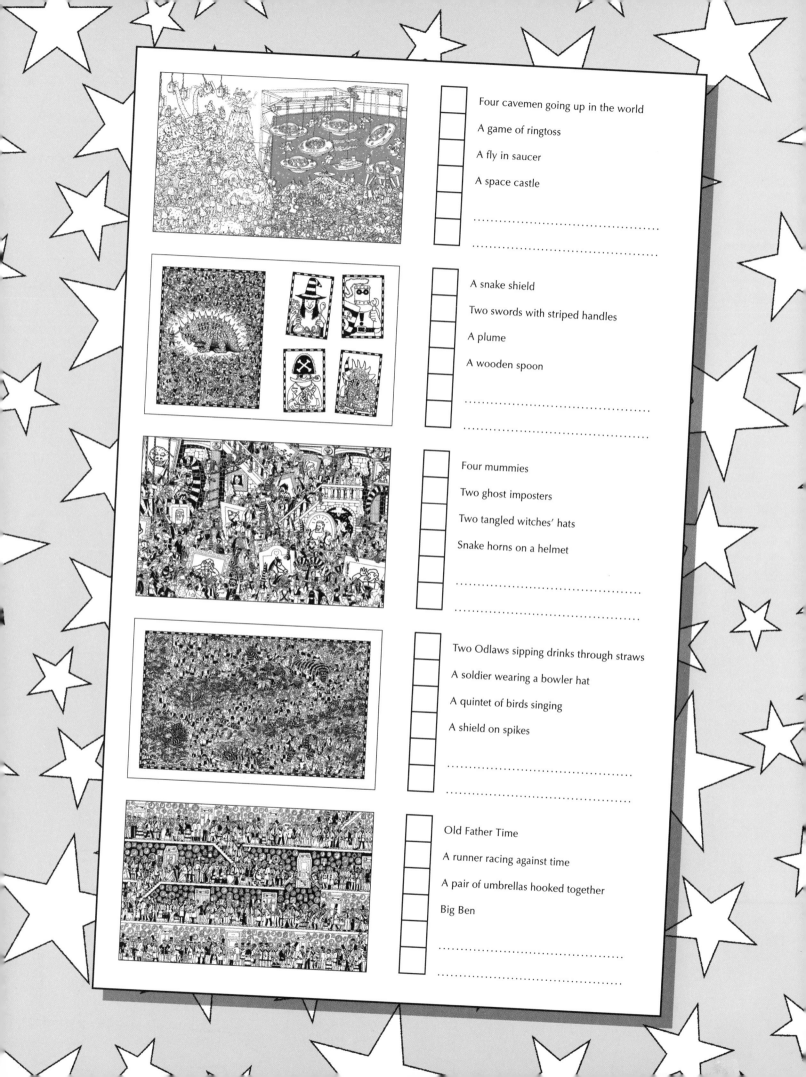

Four cavemen going up in the world

A game of ringtoss

A fly in saucer

A space castle

....
....

A snake shield

Two swords with striped handles

A plume

A wooden spoon

....
....

Four mummies

Two ghost imposters

Two tangled witches' hats

Snake horns on a helmet

....
....

Two Odlaws sipping drinks through straws

A soldier wearing a bowler hat

A quintet of birds singing

A shield on spikes

....
....

Old Father Time

A runner racing against time

A pair of umbrellas hooked together

Big Ben

....
....

The Sheriff of Nottingham

Night in armor

"Fryer" Tuck

An upside-down shield

....

....

A man wearing four hats

A spider

A woman with a clipboard

A horse-drawn wagon

....

....

Three cameras filming

A Wenda with no pockets on her skirt

A Wizard Whitebeard wearing a pom-pom hat

An Odlaw without a mustache

....

....

First U.S. edition 2016

ISBN 978-0-7636-8844-8

16 17 18 19 20 21 GCC 10 9 8 7 6 5 4 3 2 1

Printed in Borgaro Torinese, Italy

This book was typeset in Optima and Wallyfont.

Candlewick Press
99 Dover Street
Somerville, Massachusetts 02144

visit us at www.candlewick.com

AND ONE MORE THING:
Did you find
Odlaw's lost pencil?
Clue: It is black!
Happy hunting!